Footprints in Forgotten Rain

SIMON CHANDI

Dedication
To my beloved—
The one who is the heart of my poetry.
To all the lovers, the lost, the winners, the strugglers, and the dreamers.

Special Thanks

My God and Savior Jesus Christ, the one who strengthens me. I thank Him for his Agape love, support and grace.

I would like to thank everyone who was with me in my journey. If you're reading this and you helped me or supported me in any phase of my life then THANK YOU.

ISAIAH 40:31

"But they that wait upon the Lord shall renew their strength; they shall mount up with wings as eagles; they shall run, and not be weary; and they shall walk, and not faint."

ISAIAH 43:4

"Since thou wast precious in my sight, thou hast been honourable, and I have loved thee: therefore, will I give men for thee, and people for thy life."

Content

Introduction

Poetry is more than just words woven into verses—it is an unfiltered expression of the soul. *Footprints in Forgotten Rain* is a collection of emotions, experiences, and reflections that transcend time and space, inviting readers into the depths of love, loss, hope, death, sorrow and faith. Each poem in this book is a piece of my journey, an echo of my heart's deepest whispers, and a hymn to the moments that have shaped me.

In these pages, you will find the essence of human emotions—passionate love, unspoken longing, the melancholy of goodbyes, and the resilience found in faith. Some verses celebrate romance, where love lingers in the smallest details, while others capture the weight of sorrow, the search for meaning, and the strength to rise again. From the heartache of separation to the solace of divine connection, this collection paints the canvas of love with shades of joy and grief.

What makes this collection even more special is its simplicity. Each poem is crafted in a way that allows every reader—regardless of background or literary expertise—to feel the emotions in their purest form. The language is straightforward, yet the depth of feelings remains profound, ensuring that the exuberance of every moment reaches the heart of those who read it.

As you turn each page, I hope you find pieces of yourself reflected in these words. I hope my hymns become yours—your solace in solitude, your companion in reflection, and your reminder that no matter how heavy the night, the dawn always comes.

Welcome to *Footprints in Forgotten Rain*—a journey through love, loss, and the unwavering spirit of the soul.

Simon Chandi

Poems & Themes

Phase 1: Emotional Struggles & Questions on Life

1. *Life: Current Situation* (Sets the tone of inner turmoil)
2. *The Beauty of the End* (Questions life and death)
3. *What's My Mistake?* (Explores betrayal and pain)
4. *Will You?* (Introduces longing and uncertainty)

Phase 2: Love, Longing & Heartbreak

5. *The Phrase: I Love You* (Romantic suffering and loss)
6. *Permission to Forget* (Struggling to move on)
7. *A Symphony of Serenity and Loss* (Deep heartbreak)
8. *The Morning Rain* (Symbolism of love and longing)
9. *The River* (A poetic reminiscence)
10. *Sharon* (A specific love story)

Phase 3: Self-Realization & Healing

11. *My Companion* (Seeking solace in love)
12. *For You* (A declaration of love)
13. *Neer* (An emotional bond beyond romance)
14. *To The Pen* (Art as an emotional escape)
15. *The One Thing We Chase* (Moving on)

Phase 4: Finding Strength & Faith

16. *The Light I Have Yet to Know* (Introduction of faith)
17. *The Light Beyond the Storm* (Healing from emotional pain)

18. *A Father's Ode to His Daughter* (Strength in familial love)
19. *My Aurora* (A hopeful, poetic ending)
20. *Journey: Sorrow to Crown* (A triumphant conclusion)

Phase 5: Celebrating yourselves

21. Echoes Of My Heart (Acceptance, Love, Move on & memories.)
22. With God Beside Me (Celebrating Own Life)

Life- Current Situation

"An introspective poem that reflects on the struggles of existence, questioning why life feels overwhelming and difficult. The speaker seeks solace in faith, hoping for relief from suffering."

Thoughts detonate like celestial fire,

Emotions age in an urn of desire.

Each moment, I falter, on sorrow inclined,

And whisper—why was I cast into humankind?

Fate unfurls like a tempest untamed,

A battlefield where hope lies maimed.

Obscured by shadows, my dreams confined,

And still, I ask—why was I cast into humankind?

Perhaps in epochs draped in gold,

I'd stand with Akbar's council bold.

Yet grandeur wanes, like stars declined,

And still, I ask—why was I cast into humankind?

Tribulations loom in endless tide,

My sole reprieve—prayers deified.

Life's elixir turns to brackish brine,

And still, I ask—why was I cast into humankind?

Poet's note

I wrote this in a moment when everything seemed to collapse around me. The weight of expectations, responsibilities, and failures felt unbearable. But as I penned down these words, I realized that even in the darkest moments, there is always a light waiting to be found. This poem is my way of saying, "Hold on, things will change."

The Beauty Of The End

"This thought-provoking piece challenges the common fear of death, presenting it as a peaceful escape from life's chaos. It questions whether life itself is more painful than the end it leads to".

Death is beautiful,

Don't know why it is criticized.

Everything becomes unimportant when you're totally cool—

It is the process of eternal relevance, where your struggle is synthesized.

Everyone fears it, but no one has to...

As it gives you what you always wished for.

It gives you satisfaction, stuck to you via eternal separational glue.

Isn't that enough for you—to get something that you adore?

Life is the real disaster,

Stop calling it a gift.

Even you don't know when you will leave—then how can you be its master?

Death is eternal, while life moves away in a swift.

One day, you will also be taken away.

There will be tears to prove your worth.

It is a straight path to get away from this horrible play {drama of life}.

Then you will know the beauty of death, as it takes you far from kindness dearth.

Poet's note

Death has always fascinated me, not in a morbid way, but as a concept of ultimate peace. This poem is a reflection on how we often fear death while enduring the real struggles of life. In accepting death, we embrace the inevitable, finding beauty in what is beyond our control.

What's My Mistake?

"A powerful reflection on betrayal and lost trust. The poem questions why good intentions are often met with deceit and whether there is meaning behind such pain".

They say:
"You will get what you did in the past."

I say:
Then why am I stabbed in the back
By those I believed would stand with me at last?
Was my trust too blind? My faith too deep?
Did I love too hard, or did I dare to dream?

They say:
"Faith, once lost, never returns.
It is rare—like character, the higher its worth, the greater it burns."

I say:
I knocked on doors with a heart laid bare,
Bow down, they said—I did. I swear.
But all I got was empty space,
Echoes of silence and a vanished embrace.

I stood there, shattered—
A smiling, broken clown,
Wearing laughter like a mask
While my soul sank down.

They say:
"Everything happens for a reason."

I say:
Then tell me, what's the reason for betrayal's bite?
For love that fades, for friends who fight?
For promises shattered without a sound,
For trust that's buried deep underground?

But what did I do to deserve this fate?
They say, they whisper… yet never state.

Forget it—if I speak now,
They'll only sigh and complain,
"Oh Simon, you say too much again."

Poet's note

Betrayal is painful, especially when it comes from those you trust the most. This poem is my way of questioning fate, of seeking answers to why people change, why promises are broken, and why faith is sometimes misplaced.

Will You?

"Filled with doubt and vulnerability, this poem wonders if the person the speaker loves would care if they walked away. It explores the fear of being unimportant to someone we cherish".

There are so many doubts, and I don't know why.
I'm scared to find the answers—afraid they'll make me cry.

It feels like no matter how hard I make cries,
I can't seem to make things right, even after a hundred tries.

I asked, I begged, I searched for replies,
But all I received was a basket full of lies.

The train of my life is taking a turn,
And in that turn, I no longer wish to return.

I can't ignore you—your attention is the key
That brings a fleeting sense of peace to me.

But ….

But....

But tell me, what if I start to walk away?

Will you ask me **why?**

Will you **cry?**

Will you **try?**

Poet's note

Doubt and fear consume us when we question our worth in someone's life. This poem was born from that uncertainty—the fear of being forgotten, of not being fought for. It is a quiet plea to be noticed, to be valued, to be loved.

The Phrase: I Love You

Love, though beautiful, can also bring immense pain. This poem captures the agony of unfulfilled love and the heartbreak that lingers long after the words "I love you" are spoken.

Why is it hard to sit and ponder
The world's most wondrous, endless wonder?
Why must my heart endure this ache,
A love that burns yet will not break?

The only wish my soul can find
Is making her forever mine.
Yet dreams of love just make me weep,
As hope departs with every sleep.

I cry, I shout, I tear apart
The wreckage of my shattered heart.
Still, deep inside, I yearn to be
Lost with her in fantasy.

I do not know why love can be
The sweetest pain, a mystery.

Yet something tells me, soft and cruel,
That I have lost my precious jewel.

I drown in nights devoid of rest,
With grief and sorrow as my guest.
And still, she stands above them all—
My highest measure, rise and fall.

My goals are lost, my virtues blurred,
All crushed beneath one simple word.
A phrase so light, yet cut me through—
The softest whisper: **"I love you."**

Poet's note

Love, when unreciprocated or misunderstood, can be one of the most painful emotions. This poem is about the paradox of love—the way it can lift you up yet leave you broken. I wrote this after experiencing a love that left me questioning everything, wondering why something so beautiful could also cause so much pain.

Permission To Forget

"A poignant poem about the struggle to move on from a past love. Despite time passing, the memories remain, making it difficult to truly let go"

It's been years since we met,

Still, my heart beats for just a glance of your eyes...

Yes, it's been years since we met,

Yet somewhere around me, your essence lies...

Many times, I missed you—

That raven tress, full of poutiness and tantrums.

Many times, I dared to forget you—

But every time, your voice stopped me, beating around me like drums.

I still crave your zenith.

Many came, and many went, but none ever filled your place.

I pretend to forget you for the world, yet love you unhindered beneath.

How can I forget you—you, my solace?

I am fatigued by this regret.

I want to leave that reverie where I think I'll find you somewhere,

With the hope that you will meet me, at least, with a wreath.

May I have the permission to forget you, my life's heir?

Poet's note

I struggled with moving on. No matter how much time passed, the memories remained vivid, haunting me. This poem is an expression of that internal conflict—the desire to forget, yet the inability to do so. It is a plea for closure, for the strength to finally let go.

A Symphony Of Serenity & Loss

"A journey through love's beauty and the devastation of losing it. The poem reflects on cherished moments with a beloved and the emptiness that follows their absence".

I still remember the time—the sun was shining gay;

It was her eyes that made it my most beautiful day.

It wasn't beautiful merely because of her beauty;

The true reason lay in her myriad serenity.

I held her hands and felt them in every nerve of mine.

In that exact moment, I knew I had become thine.

I showed her my hymns, and her reaction was unfathomable;

To me, she became my treasured diamond, my most invaluable.

I wove words from my heart and turned them into a song,

A song that declared to the universe: I'm the one to whom she

belongs.

We wandered through eternity in my reverie—we talked, we

walked,

And she kissed my soul, her presence lighting the dark.

God gave her to me, a blessing in a bowl,

A treasure abundant, a gift to my soul.

But soon, my arcadia, my Elysium, shattered into fragments.

I felt alienated, separated, utterly lost in estrangements.

How much time does it take to forget someone—months or years?
Please, don't ask me; instead, ask my tears.

Poet's note

Falling in love was like stepping into a dream. Everything felt surreal, beautiful, eternal. But dreams do not last forever. The heartbreak that followed was unbearable, leaving me lost in the fragments of what once was. This poem is my way of holding on while learning to let go.

The Morning Rain

"A nostalgic poem that uses rain as a metaphor for emotions. It speaks of longing for someone who has drifted away, and the lingering hope that they will return".

This morning, I watched the rain—so soothing, so pure,
And guess what? My thoughts led me to you once more.

No, no, I'm not trying to forget your name,
I'm just walking my path—while you remain my train.

It feels like my moon is drifting away,
And that ache runs deep within my veins.

Don't go—just tell me if something is wrong,
I can't lose the one who, to me, is the main.

Even if the clouds take you far from sight,
I'll wait beneath the same sky, hoping for light.

I don't need answers, no perfect way,
Just let me stand beside you—come what may.

The night is long, but stars will rise,
Pain won't last—so dry your eyes.

So tell me, love, will you let me stay?
Or must I watch you drift away?

If I reach for you, will you take my hand?
Or let me fade like footprints in the sand?

Poet's note

The rain has always been symbolic for me—of renewal, of longing, of memories that refuse to fade. This poem captures the feeling of missing someone deeply, of wondering if they feel the same, of hoping for a reunion under the same sky.

The River

"A romantic poem that captures a peaceful moment shared by two people by the riverside. It reflects the purity of love and the desire to make fleeting moments last forever".

In the midst of a soulful breeze,
I prayed to God and whispered, "Please..."

Beneath the glow of a glittering sky,
The river sighed—a peaceful high.

Amidst the bloom of flowers bright,
We blushed like drizzle in soft twilight.

Sitting by the river, so serene,
Her every glance felt like a dream.
I slowly entwined my hand with hers,
A touch so warm, the world blurred.

My heart raced, lost in time,
With her presence, love felt divine.
Her laughter danced like fireflies near,
A melody only my soul could hear.

The stars above in silent grace,
Watched us share this fleeting space.
No need for words, no need for rhyme,
For love had spoken beyond time.

The night grew deep, the wind stood still,
Yet, I wished for more—my heart's own will.
I held her close, and once again,
I prayed to God with whispered pain—

"Let this moment never fade,
Let it live where dreams are made.
Freeze the night, hold back the sea,
Let time surrender... just for me."

Poet's note

There was a moment, by a river, where everything felt right. The world faded, and all that remained was her and me. This poem is a recollection of that perfect moment, a wish to freeze time and stay in that serenity forever. Everything I felt and experienced was just my imagination. Feels like I went on journey to a reverie and was never back. Honestly I don't even want to return to reality.

SHARON

"A personal story of meeting someone special, forming a deep connection, and discovering the struggles they carry. Despite differences, love persists beyond material concerns".

On the first week of semester one,
I found a girl under the burning sun.
Smiling, laughing with an innocent grace,
Wherever she went, smiles lit up the place.

We had a long conversation on casual themes,
But who knew she'd become part of my dreams?
I held her hand like she was mine—
Lost in a world beyond the bounds of time.

Then I came to know about her past,
A truth that shook me, hitting hard and fast.
She was a princess, and I wasn't rich,
Yet she loved me—like the ocean loves the beach.

I never cared if she'd stay or part;
I promised to stand by her with all my heart.

I don't know what the future will bring,
But I'll love her today, tomorrow—beyond everything

Poet's note

This poem might not be my finest work as a poet, yet it remains the most cherished piece I have ever written. Over the years, I never dared to touch it—not a single word has been altered, not a single line restructured. The reason is simple: as the words remain unchanged, so do the emotions they hold.

This poem is a fragment of time, capturing the very first moment I met her, the way she felt like sunshine in a world that had never seen such light. It traces the journey from that first conversation to the depth of emotions that followed, from the innocent joy of meeting her to the weight of knowing her past. It speaks of love beyond circumstances, beyond status, beyond the limits the world often imposes.

Though that chapter of my life has long passed—left far behind with time—it still holds meaning. It was a phase that shaped me, a story that, despite being over, remains significant. Some moments may fade, but their essence lingers, untouched by time. This poem is not just a memory; it is a testament to something beautiful, something important. And for that reason, I have never changed a word—because some things are meant to stay as they are.

My Companion

"An intimate confession of love and devotion. The speaker expresses that their beloved is not just a person in their life but a source of comfort, strength, and completeness".

Once, my beloved asked me,
"Who is your companion?"
That day, I was silent, lost in words I could not say. But now, my heart speaks through these verses, though even after all, you do not understand my love.
I wonder why… how?

In my heart, your face still shines,
Yet the distance between us makes me whine.
You are my ecstasy, my most needed need,
In this realm of anguish, grief, and woe—
You are my mimosa seed.

You said life is a journey,
More beautiful with a companion.
Then what if I tell you this? —
You are my solace, my quiet peace,
The thought that calms my restless seas.
You are my view of satisfaction,
My unhindered quest, my heart's reflection.

Carved from petals of lotus fair,
Your eyes hold all my soul lays bare.
There, in their depths, my consciousness rests,
Drifting softly in love's caress.

And after all these lines,
Do you still wish to ask me—
"Who is my companion?"

Poet's note

When someone asks who my companion is, I do not have a simple answer. But when she asked me the same this poem became my response. It speaks of a love that is more than just a relationship—it is a connection that goes beyond words, beyond circumstances. A bond that remains, even in silence.

For You

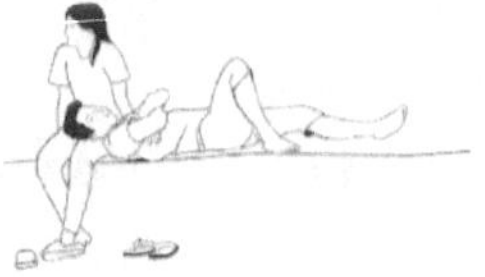

"A declaration of love and admiration, answering the questions of why the speaker loves their beloved so deeply. It emphasizes devotion and the inability to stop loving them".

The journey of pros and cons,
On which you remain an expensive lesson.
One day, my existence will turn around—
Yet I pray this lesson stays eternal.

They asked,
"What is comfort?"
I sighed,
"The quiet shelter beneath her stormy skies."

They questioned,
"Who is the owner?"
I whispered,
"The one who holds her hands when the tide dares to rise."

They demanded,
"You're hers for how long?"

I smiled,
"Until the stars forget to shine, until time unknots its ties."

They asked again, again, and again,
"Why do you love her this much?"
I replied,
"How could I not love the fire
That warms my soul yet never burns?"

They laughed,
"But what if she never stays?"
I answered,
"Even the moon doesn't stay, yet we still wait for its light."

And if fate turns cruel,
Let me be the echo of her name in the wind,
A shadow behind her footsteps,
A whisper between her dreams.

Poet's note

Love, in its purest form, is selfless. This poem is about devotion—about cherishing someone even when they do not belong to you. It is about loving someone for who they are, not for what they can give you.

NEER

"This poem speaks of an unspoken bond with a girl whose eyes hide silent sorrow. It explores the comfort and depth of a connection beyond words, where emotions are understood without explanation".

They never hid anything from me;
I wanted to see heaven, and those were the key.
Her innocent eyes never lied to me;
A fish-eyed girl tried to hide melancholy
Behind a smile as pure as Angeline.
She tried to veil them with glasses,
But they, too, were transparent and divine.

I longed to hear gratifying music,
Away from the cacophony that made me sick.
Life felt bewildered; happy moments moved like a flick.
I was frail, trapped in scuffles, cold as ice,
Yearning to heal—and I found that music in her voice.

No worries for the future, no regrets of the past;
I promised to stay with her until my breath's last.

Yes, we are together now, beyond every social caste.
We aren't in a relation but are bound by emotions.
That girl, with little brown eyes, glasses,
And short hair, is my devotion.

Poet's note

She was different. The way she looked at the world, the way she carried herself—it all fascinated me. I saw in her eyes a story she never told, a sadness she tried to mask. But in her presence, I found an unexplainable peace. This poem is about the silent connections that go beyond words, the kind that leave a mark on your soul.

To The Pen

"Dedicated to writing itself, this poem portrays how the pen becomes a medium to express deep emotions—especially love, admiration, and longing for someone special".

Oh, dear pen, shall we begin to weave,

 A tale of her-short hair, silky as eve?

Fair skin like dawn, with eyes so deep,

Where secrets of the universe seem to sleep.

I met her today, as if fate did believe.

In whispers shared, laughter took flight,

A teacher, a poet-our world felt right.

I walked her to her bus, the moments so fleet,

Her smile lingers, my heart skips its beat.

I yearn to know her beyond this twilight.

Pen, she's the muse I've longed to find,

In her presence, the chaos turns kind.

Shall I write her name in verses anew,

Or ask if she'd let me pen her view?

For her story, I'd gladly leave mine behind.

She left mid-poem, the rhyme incomplete,

A fleeting goodbye, her bus claimed the street.

But oh, pen, her voice echoes still,

A melody that bends my will.

I dream of the day when again we'll meet.

Until then, pen, let's scribble and strive,

To capture the warmth that keeps me alive.

Each word I write feels closer to her,

This bond, this spark, this gentle stir.

Shall she be the reason my poems survive?

Poet's note

As a writer, my pen is my confidant. This poem is an intimate confession to my pen, sharing the thoughts and emotions I find difficult to voice. It also captures the memory of someone I met, someone whose presence inspired poetry in me. Her departure was abrupt, yet the emotions she stirred lingered on the pages.

The One Thing We Chase

"A philosophical take on love and moving forward. It acknowledges the pain of letting go but also the necessity of growth. Love is powerful, but it is not always meant to last forever".

Love is full of odds,
wrapped in thorns that scratch and wound—
misunderstandings, distances,
fears we never say out loud.
Yet for one thing,
we risk it all—
the quiet refuge in their arms,
the warmth that melts away the chaos,
the comfort of knowing we belong.

But even the softest touch,
the gentlest presence,
cannot hold us forever.
Love soothes, love shelters,

but we are not meant to stay
where time has stopped moving.
We do not forget,
but we must move forward.

Moving on is heavier than holding on,
but it is greater too.
To let go is not to erase love,
but to outgrow what no longer fits.
And though it aches,
walking away is still
a step towards something new.

I have poured love into verses,
stitched heartbreak into poetry,
let my words carry the weight
that my heart couldn't hold.
Love has built me, broken me,
but it has never stopped me.

So live, not in yesterday, but in today.
Embrace the unwritten pages,
smile at the unknown ahead.
Because love—no matter how deep—
was never meant to be the final chapter.

Poet's note

Love is the one thing we all seek, despite the pain it brings.
This poem is about accepting that love is not meant to be

permanent—it is meant to teach us, to shape us, to lead us to new chapters. Moving on is painful, but it is also necessary.

The Light I Have Yet To Know

"Inspired by faith, this poem admires someone whose spiritual strength shines brightly. It expresses a longing to understand and embrace that same unwavering belief in God".

I see a light within your grace,
A peace that shines in quiet space.
Your heart is firm, unshaken, pure—
In Christ's strong hands, it rests secure.

I wonder how your soul can glow,
So bright in faith, so steady, slow.
Your beauty speaks in simple ways,
No need for more, no need for praise.

The way you walk with humble stride
Reflects a strength that won't subside.
I picture joy within your eyes,
Like morning sun in golden skies.

I think of words you've yet to say,
Of prayers you whisper every day.
Together, we could share His word,
Where truth in quiet hearts is stirred.

In Christ alone, we're woven tight,
A bond of faith, a guiding light.
And though your name I do not know,
In Him, our hearts still overflow.

I dream of days with Bibles near,
Where love is strong, and doubt is clear.

Poet's note

This poem was inspired by a stranger whose faith and serenity captivated me. It made me reflect on the strength that comes from unwavering belief. It is about admiration from a distance, about seeing light in someone and longing to be part of their world.

The Light Beyond The Storm

"A poem of encouragement and healing after heartbreak. It reassures the reader that they are not defined by past pain and that brighter days lie ahead".

In the shadow of heartache, you found a bitter night,
Where dreams were torn, and trust was laid to waste.
But even in the darkness, there's a hidden light—
A spark of hope, a soul that won't be chased.
And I believe in you, in the strength you've always faced.

Your heart is bruised, yet beating strong,
The past may try to keep you locked in pain.
But know—you are not defined by what went wrong.
You are not the storm; you are the break of dawn,
And in the morning light, your beauty will remain.

It's time to leave behind the echoes of his voice,
To walk a path where laughter fills the air.
For every tear, you have the power of choice—

To rise above, to heal, to repair,
And write a story where you know that someone cares.

So take my hand—we'll walk through fields of green.
The world is wide, and love is waiting here.
No one has the right to tell you who you've been.
You're the author of the life you hold so dear,
And I will stand beside you, my words sincere.

Poet's note

I wrote this for someone who had been hurt deeply, someone who deserved love but had been denied it. This poem is a promise—a reminder that no matter how broken you feel, you are not the storm. You are the dawn that follows, the light beyond the darkness.

A Father's Ode To His Daughter

A heartfelt tribute from a father to his daughter, celebrating her strength, beauty, and the love that binds them. It portrays the deep emotional connection between a parent and child.

Kept in the oyster like a pearl,
Don't let the world shun you for your curls.
Look, my beloved princess, you're not wrong—
You are the one who makes me strong.

When times are tough and everyone is gone,
You're still here, making me strong.
I may be the head of the table,
But you're the one who keeps me stable.

I've watched you grow from the cradle—
The prettiest, the sweetest, the most lovable.
You're not just good, not just better, but the best,
You've taken my melancholy and replaced it with rest.

Your first sight was sleeping on my palm,
And now, time has flown; you're my soothing calm.

I could witness the world burn, see everyone die,
But I can't bear a tear in your eye, let alone a cry.

You are the reason I continue to live—
My baby, my princess, my daughter, my smile,
The one who always makes life worthwhile.

Poet's note

*This poem is inspired by the unbreakable bond between a
father and his daughter. I have seen the love of fathers who
cherish their daughters beyond words, standing as their
protectors and guides. It is a tribute to the unwavering support
and the strength that a father finds in his child*

My Aurora

"A poem about finding light in darkness. The speaker meets someone who becomes their guiding force, bringing healing, hope, and a reason to believe in love again".

I found comfort in the desert of sorrow,
A soothing light that made pain hollow.
Relief embraced me—her magic divine,
She filled my soul and taught me to shine.

I was broken, lost, and torn apart,
As many came, made promises, then depart.
Yet she remained, my beacon so bright,
Carrying a scent like heaven's delight.

Confused, bewildered, drowning in despair,
I searched for answers, but none were there.
Then she arrived, like dawn so true,
Touching my soul, painting skies anew.

With every word, she healed my past,
A love so deep, destined to last.
She turned my silence into song,
With her, I've found where I belong.

She is the whisper in my darkest night,
The gentle hand that holds me tight.
Through every storm, through every tide,
With her, my heart will forever abide.

Poet's note

At my lowest, I found someone who brought light into my life. She did not just listen—she understood. She healed wounds I did not know I had. This poem is a dedication to her, to the warmth she brought, to the love that changed me.

Journey: Sorrow To Crown

"A poem about life's hardships and the hope that, in the end, perseverance will be rewarded. It emphasizes faith, wisdom, and resilience in overcoming life's challenges".

In this world of sorrow,
We often must borrow
The thing everyone calls joy—
Yet the moment we find it, it seems to fly.

One day on this earth, you'll see,
Fulfilment will find you, let it be.
Not by chasing perfection's race,
But through simple moments of love and grace.

Believe, my friend, and hold on tight,
One day, you'll step into the light.
Listen to wisdom, keep yourself cool,
Be wise, for the world is full of fools.

Life may seem a little long,
But it's just like a beautiful song.
Its pitch will rise, its notes may fall,
Yet sing it well, and you'll stand tall.

Through every storm and every trial,
Wear your pain with strength and style.
For in the end, when all is done,
You'll see—you were the chosen one.

Poet's note

This poem is the essence of my journey through despair and hope. I have often felt that joy is something fleeting, something borrowed rather than owned. But through my struggles, I realized that fulfillment does not come from chasing perfection but from embracing faith. Life is like a song—sometimes in tune, sometimes offbeat—but if we persevere, we will find our crown.

Echoes Of My Heart

"Poetry, for me, is not just an art—it is a pulse, a rhythm, a voice that speaks when words fail. Every line I have ever written is a fragment of my soul, a reflection of emotions too vast to be contained within silence. Love, longing, faith, despair, and resilience—each has left its mark on my heart, shaping the verses that flow from my pen. This poem is a culmination of all that I have ever felt, of every story I have carried, of the unsaid words that found a home within poetry. It is not just a poem; it is a journey—of losing, of yearning, of breaking, and of becoming whole again. And as you read, I hope you find not just my story, but yours as well."

I. The Prelude of Longing

In the quiet hush of twilight's embrace,
I whispered to the winds, seeking solace.
Carved in the hollows of my wandering heart,
A name, a touch, a memory torn apart.

I have walked the corridors of forsaken dreams,
Where laughter lingers but never redeems.
Love was a garden I once called mine,
Now overgrown with the thorns of time.

I have loved like the river loves the shore,
Only to watch the tides steal her evermore.

I have held hands I thought would stay,
Only to wake and find them washed away.

But still, my pen carves words in the dark,
Etching her absence as poetry's mark.
For though she is gone, her echoes remain,
A hymn of longing, a whisper of pain.

II. The Shattered Reflection

Once, I stood in the mirror's gaze,
Tracing the face of a boy ablaze—
A boy who dreamed, a boy who knew
That love was meant to be something true.

But love betrayed, and trust deceived,
My heart became a book of grief.
What was my crime? To give too much?
To believe in forever with just one touch?

They say the past is but a fleeting shade,
Yet why does it linger where memories fade?
Why do I bleed from wounds unseen,
From words unsaid, from love between?

I have learned to smile while breaking apart,
To laugh while burying my heart.
For no one hears a poet's cry—
Only the verses he lets slip by.

III. The Solace of Faith

But when my soul was tattered and torn,
He whispered, "My child, you were never alone."
In the silence of sorrow, in the night so deep,
I found the hands that let me weep.

Not in the arms of the world so cold,
Not in promises that cracked and broke.
But in the quiet warmth of a prayer's embrace,
Where mercy poured like gentle grace.

Jesus, my anchor, my only guide,
The refuge where my fears subside.
Though the world may take, may push, may bend,
In Him alone, I find my end.

IV. The Music of Love

Yet even in faith, I cannot deny—
Love is a melody I cannot untie.
For in the scent of the morning rain,
I still hear her voice, calling my name.

She was my dawn, my fleeting light,
A symphony of stars in the quiet night.
I wrote her in verses, in whispers, in dreams,
Yet love is never as soft as it seems.

Would she have stayed if I had spoken less?
Would she have loved me with no regrets?

But love is a traveler, it cannot be chained,
A bird that perches, then flies away even in rains.

Still, I wish for just one more dance,
One last moment, one last chance.
To tell her she was my poetry's muse,
The one hymn I never wished to lose.

V. The Resurrection of Self

But love is not the final page,
Nor sorrow's grip the end of days.
I rise again, though bruised and torn,
A soul reborn in faith's reform.

For I am more than the ones who left,
More than the ache of a heart bereft.
I am the words I dare to weave,
The light I hold, the dreams I breathe.

No longer a prisoner of love misplaced,
Nor chained by shadows I cannot erase.
I walk ahead, with scars as gold,
A heart unbroken, a spirit bold.

And if she reads these words someday,
May she know I loved in the truest way.
Not to hold, nor to claim as mine,
But to cherish, to free, and to let her shine.

For love is not about who stays or goes,
But the beauty in the love we chose.

Poet's note

"This poem was not written in a moment—it was lived through countless moments. Moments of love so deep it felt eternal, moments of loss so sharp it left scars, moments of faith so strong it became my anchor, and moments of resilience so fierce it redefined me. Each stanza is a testament to what I have felt, what I have lost, and what I have learned. I do not write to merely express; I write to connect—to touch the hearts of those who have felt the same depth of love, the same weight of sorrow, the same flicker of hope. If, in these lines, you find even a small reflection of your own emotions, then this poem has served its purpose. Because poetry, at its core, is not just about words—it is about understanding, healing, and remembering that we are never truly alone in our emotions."

With God Beside Me

Many came, many went,
Some with love, some with contempt.
They whispered lies, they cast their doubt,
Yet here I stand—unshaken, proud.

From the days of a young, bright spark,
Teaching since eleven's mark.
With lessons shared and dreams so wide,
I built a home where hope resides.

Through sleepless nights and silent cries,
Through every fall, I chose to rise.
I taught not just words, but strength and grace,
A guiding light in every space.

A thousand minds, a thousand dreams,
I shaped their wings, I fueled their beams.
And though they left to touch the sky,
They carry the fire I lit inside.

Some days were dark, the nights felt long,
But faith in God had kept me strong.

For effort pays, though patience calls,
And oh, the beauty when it falls!

I wrote through pain, I wrote through scars,
Each word a battle, each page a star.
Through every win, through every fight,
I bled in ink and found my light.

So here I stand, unbowed, untamed,
A soul once tested, now reclaimed.
With every tear and every test,
I proved to life—I give my best.

And as I walk the path ahead,
With brighter suns and storms unsaid,
I leave myself these words of mine:
"Keep writing, keep growing—with God beside."

Poet's note

This poem is not just a collection of words—it is a reflection of my journey, my struggles, and my victories. It is a tribute to the path I have walked, the storms I have endured, and the unwavering faith that has carried me through.

When I look back, I see a road filled with challenges. Many people crossed my path—some with kindness, but many with doubt, disrespect, and even falsehoods. They tried to break me, tried to bring me down with their words and actions. But I stood my ground. I refused to let their negativity define me.

*I started teaching when I was just in Class 11. At an age when most are still figuring out their own future, I was already shaping the futures of others. Teaching was not just a job for me—it was my calling, my passion. With time, I didn't just remain a teacher; I became a mentor, a guide, and eventually, an institution of my own. I built **E-Planet Academy**, my coaching center, where I have taught thousands of students over the years.*

*Every step I took was met with struggles—self-doubt, exhaustion, moments of frustration. There were days when I felt like giving up, but God never let me fall too far. I have learned that **effort doesn't always bring immediate results, but when it does, oh, what a beautiful reward it is!***

*This poem also marks a significant moment in my journey—**the completion of this book.** A book that carries not just my words, but my heart, my experiences, and my truth. Every page holds a part of me, every line speaks of a battle fought and won.*

So, I wrote this poem to celebrate myself—to remind myself of how far I have come and how much further I will go. This is my story, my resilience, my faith. And as I move forward, I leave myself with my own words:

"Keep writing, keep growing—with God beside."

Couplets

I found you in echoes of a prayer left unsaid,
A dream that lingers though the night has fled.

***

Your silence speaks in verses I cannot ignore,
Like tides that return to the same distant shore.

***

The moon watches over where my whispers lie,
Carrying your name across the midnight sky.

***

Love was never a promise carved into stone,
Yet I still wait where you left me alone.

***

Your absence lingers like an unfinished song,
A melody aching where it doesn't belong.

***

Between your words and the spaces they weave,
I lose myself in what I want to believe.

Some wounds do not bleed, some tears do not fall,
Yet they carve their names inside us all.

You held my heart like a fragile thread,
Tangled in hopes I should have shed.

***

Every goodbye you left in my skin,
Still burns like a fire that won't give in.

***

I love you in echoes, in glances, in air,
In places you've left but still linger there.

***

Your love was a whisper, fleeting and light,
Yet it stays like a shadow in every night.

***

There are stories in my ribs you'll never read,
Chapters of longing that quietly bleed.

***

The stars may not answer, but still, I confess,
My heart only speaks in your name nonetheless.

***

Some hearts don't shatter, they just fade away,
Like a forgotten sunset at the end of the day.

***

You were a season, a storm, a fleeting embrace,
Now only your echoes remain in this space.

***

Loving you was like tracing the wind,
Knowing I'd lose you, but breathing you in.

***

A love that was quiet, a love that was deep,
Now lingers in verses I struggle to keep.

***

Not all love stays, but not all love dies,
Some burn forever behind weary eyes.

***

In the hush of the night, when the whole world is still,
It is your name that my silence would fill.

***

If love was a language, then yours was the rain,
Falling, then leaving—yet whispering again.

***

About the Author

Simon Chandi is an educator, poet, and mentor whose journey is a testament to resilience and passion. His teaching career began when he was just in the 11th grade, starting with a single student. What began as a small effort soon grew into a purpose-driven mission. Despite facing betrayals from those he once called friends and overcoming countless struggles, he remained steadfast in his commitment to teaching and learning. His perseverance turned obstacles into opportunities, shaping him into the teacher he is today.

Currently, Simon teaches English at **Mission India Vidyaniketan School** and **Gram Vikas Vidyalaya**, while also running his own coaching center, **E-Planet Academy**, where he has mentored over 600 students. Beyond academics, he conducts **seminars on the importance of the English language**, helping students recognize its role in unlocking new opportunities in education and career growth.

Alongside teaching, Simon finds solace and expression in poetry. His words capture the essence of emotions, life's struggles, and unspoken thoughts. As a poet, he has contributed to various anthologies and is the author of **"Footprints in Forgotten Rain,"** a collection of poems that delve into love, loss, and the journey of self-discovery. Through his writing, he weaves experiences into verses that resonate deeply with readers.

Through all his endeavors, Simon lives by one guiding principle—one that has carried him through every challenge and success:

PROCESS – PROGRESS – PATIENCE – SUCCESS.

This mantra defines his journey, shaping both his teaching and poetic voice as he continues to inspire students and readers alike.

Dear Reader,

From the depths of my heart, thank you for taking the time to read my words. This book is more than just ink on paper—it is a reflection of emotions, experiences, and moments that shape us. I hope that in these pages, you found fragments of yourself, echoes of your own thoughts, and feelings you may have long forgotten.

If any verse, any line, or any emotion resonated with you, I ask you to share it with those who matter to you. Poetry, like love, grows when shared. Let these words reach someone who needs them—someone who might find comfort, understanding, or inspiration in them.

Your support and thoughts mean the world to me. I would love to hear from you—your reflections, your favourite pieces, and even the emotions my words stirred within you. Please share your love by leaving a review, and if you wish, let me know what topics you'd like me to explore in my next book. Your words and encouragement will shape my next journey as a writer.

Thank you once again for being a part of this journey. This is not just my story—it is ours.

With gratitude,
Simon Chandi

If love ever knocks but you're afraid to try,
If your soul still trembles with a quiet sigh,
Know that I'll be here, beyond the past,
With open arms, a love that lasts.